This book belongs to

_____

DISNEY · PIXAR

FINDING NEMO

A READ-ALOUD STORYBOOK

Adapted by Lisa Ann Marsoli
Illustrated by the Disney Storybook Artists
Designed by Disney's Global Design Group

Random House 🏠 New York

Copyright © 2003 Disney Enterprises, Inc./Pixar Animation Studios. All rights reserved under International and
Pan-American Copyright Conventions. Published in the United States by Random House Children's Books, a division of
Random House, Inc., New York, and simultaneously in Canada by Random House of Canada Limited, Toronto, in conjunction
with Disney Enterprises, Inc. RANDOM HOUSE and colophon are registered trademarks of Random House, Inc.
Library of Congress Control Number: 2002113527 ISBN: 0-7364-2126-2

www.randomhouse.com/kids/disney

Printed in the United States of America

10 9 8 7 6 5 4 3 2 1

THE DROP-OFF

At the edge of the Great Barrier Reef in Australia, a brood of clownfish was getting ready to hatch. Marlin and Coral, the mother and father, proudly watched over their eggs in the grotto.

"We still have to name them," Coral said. "I like Nemo."

Suddenly, a barracuda appeared. Marlin rushed to protect Coral, but the barracuda's tail knocked him out cold.

Marlin awoke to an eerie silence. When he swam to the grotto, he found only one tiny egg—injured but still okay.

"There, there, there. It's okay. Daddy's here," Marlin said softly, cradling the egg in his fin. "I promise I will never let anything happen to you . . . Nemo," he whispered to the egg.

From that day on, Marlin was very
protective of his son—especially since
Nemo was born with a "lucky" fin. It was
smaller than his other fin and made him
an awkward swimmer. When it
was time for Nemo to start
school, Marlin didn't want to
let his son go.

But Nemo couldn't wait!

"Dad, how old are sea turtles?"
Nemo asked on the way to school.

"Well, if I ever meet a sea turtle,
I'll ask him," Marlin said.

At school, Nemo climbed on the back
of the teacher, Mr. Ray.

To his horror, Marlin learned that Mr. Ray was taking the class on a trip to the Drop-off—the very cliff where Coral and the eggs had been attacked!

"Come on, Nemo!" Nemo's new friends sneaked away from the rest of the class. At the edge of the Drop-off, they dared each other to swim up and touch a boat anchored nearby. "How far can you go?" Tad, one of Nemo's classmates, said to the clownfish.

Just then, Marlin swam over. "Nemo! No!" he cried.

"Dad, I wasn't gonna go—" Nemo said, starting to explain.

"You think you can do these things, but you just can't!" his father said angrily.

"I hate you," Nemo mumbled.

Mr. Ray heard the commotion and
swam over to help. While Marlin was
busy talking to the teacher, Nemo swam
to the boat and touched it with his fin.
He was tired of his dad thinking he was
too little and too weak to do anything!

When Marlin heard Nemo's classmates shouting, he looked out toward the boat. "Nemo!" he cried as a diver swam up right behind his son.

"Swim, Nemo, swim!" the kids called.

"Daddy! Help me!" Nemo cried as the diver scooped him up.

But before Marlin could do anything, the diver—and Nemo—was already on the boat. There was no way Marlin could catch up!

Marlin swam to a busy underwater passage.
"Has anybody seen a boat? They took my son!"
he cried.

Finally, a regal blue tang fish named Dory told
him she had seen a boat. "Follow me!" she said.

But Dory had a problem: she couldn't remember
anything for more than a few minutes. When she
turned and saw Marlin, she got angry with him.
"Stop following me, okay?" she exclaimed.

Suddenly, a big shark named Bruce showed up.

Bruce took Dory and Marlin
to a sunken submarine. Inside
was a meeting of sharks who
claimed to be vegetarians. Marlin
didn't trust them.

But then Marlin spotted a diving mask—
just like the one worn by the diver who had captured
Nemo! "What do these markings mean?" he wondered
aloud. "I don't read human."

Suddenly, Bruce was overcome with hunger. He chased
Dory and Marlin through the submarine, snapping his jaws.

The pair raced into a tube that held a torpedo.

Marlin and Dory lodged the torpedo
in Bruce's mouth to
escape. The shark
spit it out, and
seconds later,
it exploded!

Meet the Tank Gang

Far away, a giant hand dropped Nemo into unfamiliar waters. Several friendly but strange fish surrounded him. Bubbles, Peach, Jacques, Bloat, Deb, and Gurgle introduced themselves. Nemo was in a fish tank in a dentist's office! The other fish were thrilled to meet Nemo—a fish from the open sea!

Nigel, a pelican, flew to the window to say hello to his tank friends. The dentist, Dr. Sherman, shooed him away, knocking over a framed picture. Then Nemo learned his fate: the little clownfish was going to be given to Darla, Dr. Sherman's bratty niece . . . who had shaken her last fish to death!

Then Nemo met the leader of the tank, Gill. Nemo noticed that Gill had a damaged fin, too, and felt a special bond with his new friend.

That night, the tank fish held a ceremony to accept Nemo into their group.

Gill nicknamed Nemo Shark Bait and shared his plan for how they would all escape from the tank—a plan that depended on little Nemo!

Meanwhile, Marlin woke after the torpedo's explosion. He and Dory were right on the edge of a deep trench. To make matters worse, Dory accidentally dropped the diver's mask!

As they swam down after the mask to darker waters, a glowing orb appeared. It was attached to a hungry anglerfish! While Marlin struggled with the fierce angler, Dory used the fish's light to see the writing on the mask. "P. Sherman, 42 Wallaby Way, Sydney," she read.

After they escaped from the angler, Dory asked a school of moonfish to give her directions to Sydney. Marlin had already started swimming away when one of the moonfish gave Dory a tip. "When you come to a trench, swim *through* it, not *over* it," he warned her.

Soon Marlin and Dory reached the trench. But instead of swimming through it as Dory had suggested, Marlin convinced her to swim over it. They were instantly surrounded by a forest of jellyfish. How would they ever escape?

"All right. Here's the game!" Marlin cried. "Whoever can hop the fastest out of these jellyfish wins. You can't touch the tentacles— only the tops."

Dory had almost made it through when she got stung. Marlin pulled her free, but not before he was stung, too.

Back in the fish tank, Gill gave Nemo swimming lessons while the two swapped stories.

Gill caught Nemo looking at his biggest scar. "My first escape—landed on dental tools," Gill told him. "I was aiming for the toilet. All drains lead to the ocean, kid."

Later, the fish began the first step of their escape plan: get the tank dirty. If they could break the filter, Dr. Sherman would have to clean the tank—and that would mean removing the fish and putting them in plastic bags. While the bags were on the counter, the fish would roll themselves out the window to freedom.

Coached by Gill, Nemo swam into the filter and wedged a pebble in the rotating fan.

But the pebble came loose and Nemo was sucked toward the sharp blades. The other fish rescued him, but Nemo was terrified.

The escape plan was ruined—and Gill realized he had put Nemo in danger.

KEEP SWIMMING

Meanwhile, some sea turtles had rescued Marlin and Dory after their dangerous encounter with the jellyfish. "Takin' on the jellies—awesome!" Crush, a surfer turtle, proclaimed.

Marlin told the younger turtles the story of his quest to find his son. Soon the tale was being passed throughout the ocean from sea creature to sea creature, until Nigel overheard the news from another pelican.

Nigel rushed back to the dentist's office to tell Nemo that Marlin was on his way.

Inspired by his father's bravery, Nemo grabbed a pebble and rushed over to the filter. He successfully jammed it into the fan.

"Shark Bait, you did it!" the tank gang cheered.

They had two days until Dr. Sherman's niece arrived. Now that the filter was broken, would the tank get dirty enough to need a cleaning by then?

Out in the ocean,
Marlin and Dory bid the sea
turtles good-bye. Marlin called,
"Crush! How old are you?"
He couldn't wait to tell Nemo
the answer when he saw him.

Marlin and Dory swam and swam until they were lost. Dory asked a blue whale for directions, but they were sucked into its humongous mouth.

Just when it looked like things couldn't get any worse, the water inside the whale's mouth began to drain into its stomach!

Back in the tank, Nemo and his friends felt their luck was changing for the better. Without a working filter, the tank was a nice, slimy green.

Dr. Sherman swiped his finger across the inside of the glass. "Crikey!" he said with disgust. "I'd better clean the fish tank before Darla gets here."

The tank gang rejoiced.

"Are you ready to see your dad, kid?" Gill asked Nemo.

"Uh-huh!" Nemo cried happily.

The next morning when the fish woke up, the water was perfectly clear. The tank had already been cleaned by a brand-new, high-tech filter called the Aqua Scum 2003! The dentist would never have to clean the tank again.

"Boss must have installed it last night while we were sleeping," guessed Gill. The fish realized that their escape plan was ruined again.

"Wh—what are we gonna do?" Nemo asked, panicking.

Not far away, in Sydney Harbor, a blue whale surfaced and spouted. Riding atop the spray were Marlin and Dory!

"Dory! We made it!" Marlin cried joyfully. "We're going to find my son! All we have to do is find the boat that took him." The problem was, there were boats as far as the eye could see. Suddenly, a pelican swooped down and scooped them up.

The pelican landed on the dock, threw its head back, and prepared to enjoy its catch. "I didn't come this far to be breakfast!" Marlin cried. He and Dory stubbornly wedged themselves sideways in the bird's throat.

Nigel, perched nearby, watched as the choking pelican stumbled around the dock. Nigel raced over and whacked him on the back.

Marlin and Dory flew out of the pelican's mouth. As he flopped helplessly on the dock, Marlin said with a gasp, "I've got to find my son, Nemo!"

Nigel couldn't believe it. "He's that fish that's been fighting the whole ocean!" he exclaimed.

By this time, a flock of hungry seagulls had gathered. "Mine! Mine! Mine!" they shouted.

"Hop inside my mouth if you want to live," whispered Nigel.

Marlin and Dory jumped inside Nigel's beak, and they were off. The seagulls followed, but Nigel's tricky maneuvers led the birds smack into a boat's sail.

THE GREAT ESCAPE

Back at the dentist's office, Dr. Sherman stuck a net into the tank and captured Nemo. "Jump in and swim down!" Gill yelled. The rest of the tank gang joined Nemo in the net and forced it away from the dentist.

But suddenly, Dr. Sherman scooped Nemo into a plastic bag. Then he set the plastic bag by the tank.

"Roll, kid, roll!" the others cried. Nemo swam furiously back and forth. But the dentist spotted the wobbly bag and stuck it in a tray to keep Nemo from falling. Nemo and his friends were worried. Darla would be arriving any minute!

Suddenly, a bell rang!
Darla burst into the
room. "Fishy! Fishy!
Fishy!" the dentist's
niece cried.

Dr. Sherman reached for the
bag. Inside, Nemo was floating
upside down—playing dead! Everyone in
the tank cheered. If the dentist flushed Nemo
down the toilet, he'd travel through the plumbing to
freedom! But their joy instantly turned to horror when
Dr. Sherman started walking Nemo over to the trash
can instead!

Just then, Nigel showed up on the window ledge and flew inside. The dentist dropped Nemo's bag onto a sharp dental tool. The bag began to leak. Nemo spotted Darla and played dead.

Marlin peeked out of Nigel's mouth—and saw Nemo floating upside down. He feared the worst.

Dr. Sherman pushed Nigel back outside and shut the window.

Darla picked up Nemo's bag and shook it. Gill knew he had to do something. The other tank fish launched Gill out of the aquarium, and he landed right on Darla's forehead!

Nemo fell out of the hole in the bag and onto a dental mirror on the tray. Gill flipped himself from Darla's forehead onto the tray. "Tell your dad I said hi," he said—and then he smacked his tail on the dental mirror, causing Nemo to fly over Darla's head and into the spit sink. Nemo escaped down the drain!

Back in the harbor, Nigel dropped Marlin and Dory into the sea. Overcome with sadness, Marlin said good-bye to Dory. She pleaded to stay with him— he had become like family to her.

But it was no use. Marlin couldn't stand to be around any reminder of his failed search for his son. He swam off and began his long journey home.

Meanwhile, Nemo rode the rapids through the water treatment plant. When he finally poked his head out into daylight, he was greeted by two hungry crabs perched on the pipe. Nemo quickly swam away to avoid their snapping claws. He had just missed his dad passing by.

Escaping from the crabs, Nemo swam
back toward the harbor and went off in
search of his father. But instead, he found
Dory swimming in circles and sobbing.

Dory and Nemo
introduced themselves to
each other—but of course Dory
had no memory of Nemo or the
search she had been on to find him.
Nevertheless, the two swam off together.

Luckily, Dory spotted the word "Sydney" on the water treatment pipe—and suddenly remembered everything. She led Nemo back to where she had last seen Marlin.

Dory described Nemo's dad and asked the crabs if they had seen him. They wouldn't talk—until she threatened to turn them into seagull food!

"All right, I'll talk," one of the crabs cried. "He went to the fishing grounds!"

Dory and Nemo were reunited with
Marlin in the fishing grounds nearby. Before
they had a chance to celebrate, an enormous net
swept up Dory along with a huge school of groupers.

Thinking quickly, Nemo said, "Let's tell every fish
to swim down!"

Nemo swam inside the net to help. "Swim down!" Marlin cried—and soon all the fish had broken through the net. But where was Nemo?

Dory and Marlin found him beneath the net. Marlin was relieved when Nemo's eyes fluttered open. "Dad, I'm sorry. I don't hate you," Nemo said.

"Oh, thank goodness!" Marlin cried. "And guess what? I met a sea turtle. They live to be a hundred and fifty years old!"

Weeks later, Marlin and Nemo raced to school. They had some amazing tales to tell—but most of their friends didn't believe them. Then Bruce and the other sharks showed up with Dory. Everyone's mouths hung open as the giant sharks greeted Marlin.

Nemo swam onto Mr. Ray's back, and the
class started to leave. "Oh, wait! I forgot
something," Nemo said.

Nemo swam back to his dad and gave him
a big hug. "Love ya, Dad," said Nemo.

"I love you, too, son," said Marlin.